anythink

SCOOB

MINI MYSTERIES

REDBEARD'S REVENGE

by John Sazaklis   Illustrated by Christian Cornia

PICTURE WINDOW BOOKS
a capstone imprint

Published by Picture Window Books, an imprint of Capstone.
1710 Roe Crest Drive
North Mankato, Minnesota 56003
capstonepub.com

Library of Congress Cataloging-in-Publication Data
Names: Sazaklis, John, author. | Cornia, Christian, 1975- illustrator
Title: Redbeard's revenge / by John Sazaklis;
illustrated by Christian Cornia.
Description: North Mankato, Minnesota : Picture Window Books,
[2021] | Series: Scooby-Doo! mini mysteries | Audience: Ages 5-7 |
Audience: Grades K-1 | Summary: "The members of Mystery Inc. set
sail on a spooky search for the ghost of the pirate Redbeard. Can they
trap the pirate ghost, or will he get his revenge? Scooby-Doo and gang
are hoping to crack the case before they have to walk the plank in
this chapter book mystery!"—Provided by publisher.
Identifiers: LCCN 2021002829 (print) | LCCN 2021002830 (ebook)
ISBN 9781663910028 (hardcover) | ISBN 9781663921307 (paperback) |
ISBN 9781663909992 (ebook pdf)
Subjects: CYAC: Mystery and detective stories. | Ghosts—Fiction. |
Pirates—Fiction. | Great Dane—Fiction. | Dogs—Fiction.
Classification: LCC PZ7.S27587 Rd 2021 (print) | LCC PZ7.S27587
(ebook) | DDC [E]—dc23
LC record available at https://lccn.loc.gov/2021002829
LC ebook record available at https://lccn.loc.gov/2021002830

Design Element: Shutterstock/natashanast,
cover and back cover background

Designer: Tracy Davies

TABLE OF CONTENTS

MEET THE MYSTERY INC. GANG!

SHAGGY

Norville "Shaggy" Rogers is a laid-back dude who would rather search for food than clues . . . but he usually finds both!

SCOOBY-DOO

A happy hound with a super snout, Scooby-Doo is the mascot of Mystery Inc. He'll do anything for a Scooby Snack!

FRED

Fred Jones, Jr. is the oldest member of the group. Friendly and fun-loving, he's a good sport—and good at them too.

DAPHNE

Brainy and bold, the fashion-forward Daphne Blake solves mysteries with street smarts and a sense of style.

VELMA

Velma Dinkley is clever and book smart. She may be the youngest member of the team, but she's an old pro at cracking cases.

MYSTERY MACHINE

Not only is this van the gang's main way of getting around, but it is stocked with all the equipment needed for every adventure.

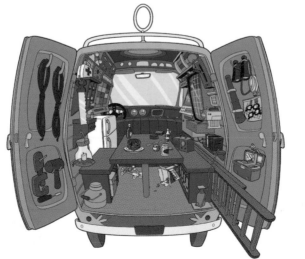

CHAPTER ONE
REDBEARD APPEARS

The Mystery Inc. gang pulled up to a huge mansion and piled out of the Mystery Machine. They had been called by Mr. Magnus, the shipping tycoon, to crack a case.

A butler opened the huge door. They followed him into Magnus Manor.

Mr. and Mrs. Magnus were in a state of shock.

"The cargo has been stolen from his ships," Mrs. Magnus said.

"It was Redbeard!" Mr. Magnus yelled. "I saw him with my own eyes!"

"Redbeard?" Velma asked. "The legendary pirate from hundreds of years ago?"

"That would mean you saw a ghost," Fred said.

"Like, did he say g-ghost?" Shaggy asked Scooby-Doo.

The gang went to the dock to investigate. A worker pointed out the ship that belonged to Mr. Magnus.

"We've got a job to do," Daphne said. "Let's go!"

Just then, a mysterious fog rolled in. It covered the dock and made the ship hard to see.

All of a sudden, the ship began to glow with an eerie light!

The Mystery Inc. gang climbed aboard the empty ship. **THUMP! THUMP! THUMP!** They heard the sound of a wooden leg.

Suddenly, a scary-looking pirate appeared.

"ARGH!"

CHAPTER TWO

THE PESKY PIRATE

"ZOINKS!" Shaggy shouted. "Like, it's Redbeard!"

"And re's really real!" Scooby-Doo said, panicked.

The members of Mystery Inc. ran away as fast as they could.

The ghost ship was full of twists and turns.

"Jeepers!" Daphne said. "I found a room full of costumes!"

"And weapons," added Fred.

The gang dressed and grabbed some weapons.

"We are ready for that red-headed robber," Velma said.

"Like, now we can catch Redbeard red-handed!" Shaggy added.

"I have a groovy idea, gang," Fred said. "Let's split up and search the spooky ship."

Daphne and Velma went one way. Scooby and Shaggy went another. Fred was left all alone.

"Hmm," Fred said to himself. "Guess it wasn't such a groovy idea."

Suddenly, Redbeard appeared and grabbed Fred.

"AHOY, MATEY!" cried the crook. "You're mine!"

Shaggy and Scooby-Doo heard a strange noise.

CLANK! CLANK! CLANK!

They climbed to the deck and saw Fred walking the plank!

"RUH-ROH!" screamed Scooby.

The pesky pirate appeared behind
the duo.

"ZOINKS!" shouted Shaggy.

"Quit blubberin' ye landlubbers!"
growled the ghost.

CHAPTER THREE

BUBBLE TROUBLE

Redbeard took the frightened friends to the galley. The creepy crook made them cook for him.

Scooby-Doo poured lots and lots of lemon juice into the pot. But it was really lemon-scented soap!

The room filled with big, soapy
bubbles. Redbeard was trapped!

Daphne and Velma found their
friends and aimed their weapons.

POP! CRASH!

Redbeard landed hard on the floor. His mask popped off.

"It's Mr. Magnus!" Shaggy shouted.

"**JINKIES!**" Velma said. "There was no greedy ghost!"

"Mr. Magnus kept the cargo instead of giving it to the owners," added Daphne.

"And I would have gotten away with it," yelled Mr. Magnus, "if not for you meddling kids!"

An officer arrived to take the terrible tycoon away.

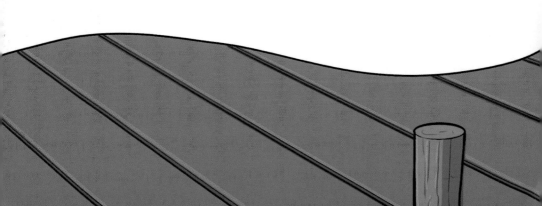

"Another mystery solved by Mystery Inc.," Fred said.

"A job well done," Velma agreed.

"That's right!" Dahpne said.

"Like, I think it's time we set sail for home," Shaggy said.

Scooby agreed.

"SCOOBY-DOOBY-DOO!"

GLOSSARY

cargo—objects carried by a ship, aircraft, or other vehicle

galley—the kitchen on a ship

landlubber—someone who is not familiar with the sea

legendary—well known

meddle—to interfere with someone else's business

pesky—annoying

plank—a long board that goes off the side of a ship; similar to a diving board

tycoon—a person who has great power, influence, and wealth

AUTHOR

John Sazaklis is a *New York Times* best-selling author with almost 100 children's books under his utility belt! He has also illustrated Spider-Man books, created toys for *MAD* magazine, and written for the BEN 10 animated series. John lives in New York City with his superpowered wife and daughter.

ILLUSTRATOR

Christian Cornia is a character designer, illustrator, and comic artist from Modena, Italy. He has created artwork for publishers, advertisers, and video games. He currently teaches character design at the Scuola Internazionale di Comics of Reggio Emilia. Christian works digitally but remains a secret lover of the pencil, and he doesn't go anywhere without a sketchbook in his bag.

TALK ABOUT IT

1. The Mystery Inc. gang is often chasing ghosts. Do you believe in ghosts? Why or why not?

2. Do you think it was a good idea for the team to split up? What would you have done?

3. What would have happened if the team hadn't caught the pirate ghost?

WRITE ABOUT IT

1. Make a list of people you would want on your mystery-solving team. Next to each name add a reason you want that person on your team.

2. Would you rather be part of a team or solve a mystery on your own? Write a few sentences about your answer.

3. Write a short story featuring your favorite members of the Mystery Inc. team. Put them in an adventure or have them solve a mystery!

Help solve mystery after mystery with Scooby-Doo and the gang!

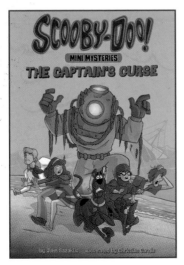

NEW TITLES!